Friday Morning Blues

Written by Danielle Prejean

Inquiries should be addressed to:Essenceexpressions4@gmail.com

Website: www.essenceexpressions.square.site

Barcode: PDF: PDF: https://www.myidentifiers.com/isbn_assets/barcodes/

2056283/9780578320281/9780578320281_10-00_ean.pdf

ISBN: 978-0-578-32028-1

Library of Congress Catalog

Published by: EssenceExpressions

Paperback edition: 2021

To my readers,

No matter what you want out of life, you must put in the work. First, believe in yourself without a doubt. Loved ones can encourage and motivate you, but those words mean nothing if you don't believe it yourself first. Nothing will come to those who doubt their abilities. Instead of worrying about how things can go wrong, just think of how things can go right! Speak and thinking positive about what you aspire to achieve whether academically or in life's journey and watch it manifest. Self-doubt and stress will happen, but you must not let it overtake you. You must fight it! Be consistent. Be content. Be positive and enjoy the process. You won't always get the grade you want or pass the test, and that's okay. See where you went wrong and try it again. Practice some more, learn what you could have done better, and never give up. Just remember that with failure comes success. After it rains, a beautiful rainbow appears. There is light at the end of the tunnel-just focus on what's important to you and work at it!

Sincerely,

Danielle Prejean

About the
Author

Danielle Prejean is a former graduate from The Prairie View A&M University, where she holds a degree in Education. She debuts her first book called "Friday Morning Blues", which inspired her through the struggle and hardship of getting through test anxiety throughout the years. She believes it is imperative to speak positivity within yourself and be amongst others who believe in you. Her goal is to be able to bring awareness and real life connections through her lens and be able to share it with the world.

I dashed off to school Monday morning with excitement to find out that my favorite third grade teacher, Ms. Berry, was out for the day and grumpy old Ms. Steeple would teach our class.

Ms.Steeple was an old gray-haired lady with a mole on her cheek the size of a gumball. She lived alone in a creepy old house with a dozen cats, and everyone disliked her.

Ms.Steeple gave us instruction on what she expected of us and the assignments that we must complete by the end of the school day. Things couldn't get any worse!

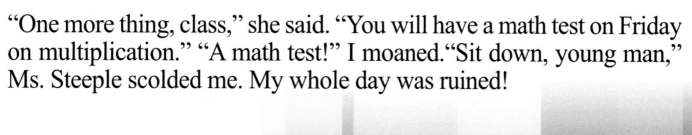

"One more thing, class," she said. "You will have a math test on Friday on multiplication." "A math test!" I moaned. "Sit down, young man," Ms. Steeple scolded me. My whole day was ruined!

During lunch time, I didn't eat. My stomach was in knots, but I didn't know why. I sat there quietly, thinking about the math test on Friday.
"What's wrong, Jaycen?" asked Camron.
"I'm not very good at tests."
"Don't think about it too much. You will do great. I'm sure of it," he assured me.

That was easier said than done. He was great at taking tests. What did he know? The day was almost over, and I had to think of an excuse to miss the test on Friday. Maybe I could say I was sick, or maybe I could be a fly on the wall. So much to think about and so little time!

I returned to school the next day feeling with lots of emotions running through my head. I couldn't focus on anything else. Ugh, I just wanted it to be over! Before the bell rang, I rushed to Ms. Berry's arms and cried.

"Jaycen, what's wrong?" she asked.

"I'm not confident in taking the test on Friday," I told her.

"Take a deep breath. Relax." She smiled at me. "You are smart, Jaycen. You have excellent grades. This test will not determine your success."
I looked at her, still worried.
"I understand how you are feeling," she said kindly.
"You do?"
"It's completely normal. You are experiencing test anxiety."
I had never heard of that before.

"What is test anxiety, Ms. Berry?"

"Test anxiety is when you feel worried about a test. It is like performance anxiety, when you are worried about doing well on a specific task. You don't want to worry about failing an exam before you take it, because it might just happen. Whatever energy you put into it, whether it's positive or negative, that's the result you will receive. If you want to change that, you have to change the way you think and speak."

"I don't understand," I said.

"I experience test anxiety too," Ms. Berry told me. "Anxiety can happen to anyone of any age. When I was in college, I had to take a test to pass the class. My stomach was in knots and all I could think about was the test. My hands were sweating and I could barely eat. That was not the only time it happened to me, either. I experienced it before every test, and I knew I had to do something about it. I had to learn to handle my anxiety so it wouldn't control me anymore."

"Did you pass your test, Ms. Berry?" I asked tearfully.
"Yes, I did," she answered with a smile.
"How?"

"First, I had to take a deep breath and relax. I knew I could perform well on the test. I told myself, 'I can do this. I am smart, and I will not let this test defeat me.' I had to use positive thoughts so I could feel confident about taking the test." I nodded, waiting for her to go on.

"Second, it was important for me to develop an efficient study plan to keep track of my progress. I decided when I would study each day and for how long. I also studied with a partner, because two heads are better than one. I knew I had to study efficiently and be consistent, using all the materials my professor provided for me in order to successfully pass the test."

I nodded. It made sense. Maybe I could do that too!

"Getting sleep is very important too. I needed at least eight hours of sleep so my mind could be energized and ready to go. Without proper sleep, I couldn't function well or remember what I had studied." Ms. Berry smiled at me.

"Go in with confidence. Think positive thoughts and don't let anyone or anything ruin the process. I know you can pass this test. You are smart, and you won't let this test defeat you. Take a deep breath and tackle it. You got this!"

"Thank you, Ms. Berry," I said. "That really helped me. I have been stressing about this test, but I could spend that time studying instead." "You're welcome, Jaycen! Remember to always stay positive and study efficiently in order to receive the results that you want."

The bell rang for Ms. Berry to get the class from the cafeteria. I had a smile on my face while I walked with her. It was a smile of relief because now I knew what I was feeling. I knew what I had to do to pass my test on Friday. Things would go smoothly-at least I thought they would!

"Rise and shine," my mom said. "It's time to get up for school."
"Mom, I don't want to go today."
"Why not, honey?"
"I just don't feel like going, that's all."
"Well, Jaycen, that's not an excuse to stay home from school."
She came in to feel my forehead. "Is there something bothering you?"
My heart said yes, but my mind said no.

"No, nothing is bothering me."

"Okay, I'll be in the car in fifteen minutes." My mom closed the bedroom door.Ugh. I pulled the covers over my face, wishing I could hide under a rock until all of this blew over, but I knew I couldn't. Fifteen minutes later, Mom honked the car horn. "You're going to be late!" We arrived at school and I walked with my head down, trying to pull myself together.

"Hey, Jaycen!"
I turned around to see Camron walking toward me. I tried my best to avoid him, but he talked to me anyway. He could be annoying. All he talked about was nerdy stuff, and then he brought up the math test and I immediately cringed.

"Are you ready for the test, Jaycen?"
I wanted to yell at the top of my lungs, but all I could say was, "Yes."
We headed to the cafeteria to wait for Ms. Berry to come get us.

That night, I studied and practiced my math for an hour before bed. I felt prepared and ready to take on the test, but my hands began to sweat again just thinking about it. "I can do this," I said. "I am smart, and I will not let this test defeat me!"

Then I said it again. "I can do this. I am smart, and I will not let this test defeat me."
I yawned and climbed into bed, thinking about the test. Thank goodness Ms. Berry helped me with my anxiety!

It was finally the big test day, and I felt great! I'd gotten a good night' s rest and my mind was at ease.

"Jaycen, how are you this morning?" Mom asked as I came into the kitchen for breakfast.

"Mom, I feel happy and prepared to tackle this math test," I said proudly.

She smiled. "I'm so proud of you, my dear.

I want you to know that you are intelligent and capable of accomplishing anything you set your mind to. Never give up! Keep pushing and break through whatever tries to stop you, because success lies on the other side of doubt. If you second guess yourself, doubt yourself, or just simply give up, how will you know what's waiting for you? You have the knowledge and skills to pass. Stay consistent and study. Everything else will fall right into place, my dear."

The bell rang, and we were all seated. The class was quiet. No one made a sound.

"Okay, class, put everything away and under your desk," Ms. Berry said. "You should only have a pencil and a sheet of scratch paper out. Remember to take your time. This is not a race. You have forty-five minutes to complete your test. Show plenty of work and double check your answers. You may start. Good luck!"

Ms. Berry monitored the class, gracefully walking through each aisle. I stared at my test and instantly started to sweat. There were twenty multiplication facts to complete. This was not good. This was not good at all! My first problem was 7x4=?

Uh-oh! My mind went completely blank. I felt someone staring at me. I looked out of the corner of my eye and there she was. Ms. Berry stared at me with a stern look.

I pretended I was solving a problem in my head. I strained my eyes to see if she was still looking at me, and she was.

She said, "Make sure you are not looking at anyone else's test, but your own."

Oh gosh, had she seen me? If I didn't get my act together, I wouldn't pass this test. If only this day had never come. I had to take a deep breath and calm down.

I wrote my multiples of 7 and counted each multiple until I reached the fourth one. My product was 28.

I double checked my answer and counted 7 groups of 4. It was the same! I was on a roll now, and everything came back to me. I just had to stay calm and positive. Everything would work out for those who believed it.

I finished my test before time was up. What a relief! I double checked my work and waited patiently until Ms. Berry called us to stop.

"Everyone put your pencils down. Time is up. I will grade your test over the weekend and you will see your grade on Monday."

My weekend would be smooth sailing. I knew I passed my test!

"Good morning, everyone," Ms. Berry said on Monday. "I graded your tests and put them in the system just in time for your report cards on Thursday."

I bounced in my seat as Ms. Berry walked around, placing everyone's graded tests face-down on their desks. My hands started to sweat again. I was eager to see what damaged I had done. I replayed every question in my head as Ms. Berry moved closer to me.

Looking at some of my classmates' faces, I knew I was doomed. My head hit the desk. I just wanted this Monday to be over with. Ms. Berry tapped me on the shoulder and smiled as she placed my test on the desk.

Maybe it wasn't as bad as I thought.

WOW!
I passed! I couldn't believe what I was seeing. I couldn't wait to go home and show my mother.
My insides cried tears of joy. I had defeated my anxiety, and I knew I could do it again!

"Mom!" I yelled when I got home.
"Yes, dear?"
"Look! Look!"
"What is it, Jaycen?"
"I passed my math test!"

Mom smiled at me. "I knew you could do it. All it took was believing in yourself and having faith that you can do anything you put your mind to. When you ask, you shall receive. We have to celebrate your accomplishment!"

"Oh boy! Can we have pizza and ice cream?"
Mom laughed. "Sure, why not!"
We ended the night with a large pepperoni pizza with hamburger and bacon toppings and a bowl of my favorite strawberry ice cream. Yummy!

Made in the USA
Columbia, SC
05 May 2022

60026548R00024